Bonnwit Kabrit

a Haitian bedtime story

Elizabeth Turnbull

Illustrated by Erin Vaganos

Light Messages

Elizabeth Turnbull
elizabeth@lightmessages.com
eturnbull.lightmessages.com

Illustrated by Erin Vaganos

Published by Light Messages Publishing
Printed in the United States of America
ISBN: 978-1-61153-064-3

For Simeon, my godson

IN THE LAKOU STANDS A HUT
GUARDED BY A SLEEPY PUP.

INSIDE, THE GRANMOUN
SLEEPS ON A MAT.

AT HIS FEET PURRS A CALICO CHAT.

THE BOUGAINVILLEA CLIMBS THE STONE WALL.

BENEATH iTS PiNK FLOWERS hiDES a SOCCER BALL.

Down By The Sea,

A ZANDOLIT SCURRIES ALONG THE BANNAN TREE.

THE WAVES FROM LANMÈ GREET THE SHORE,

AND A CRAB ASKS
HER MOTHER
FOR FIVE MINUTES MORE.

SNUGGLED BENEATH THE STARRY SKY,
THE KABRIT UTTERS A LITTLE SIGH.

THE PATCHWORK MOUNTAINS
STAND TALL AND PROUD
"Shhh," THEY WHISPER, "NOT TOO LOUD."

COME ALONG, MY CHILD. IT'S TIME TO SLEEP.

ONE BY ONE,

WE'LL SAY BONNWIT.

BONNWIT LAKOU.

BONNWIT PUP.

BONNWIT GRANMOUN
WHO SLEEPS ON A MAT,

AND BONNWIT TO THE CALICO CHAT.

BONNWIT BOUGAINVILLEA
WHO CLIMBS THE STONE WALL.

BONNWiT TO THE hiDDEN SOCCER BALL.

BONNWIT ZANDOLIT
ON THE BANNAN TREE.

BONNWiT WAVES WHO gREET ThE ShORE.

BONNWIT TO THE CRAB
WHO WANTS FIVE MINUTES MORE.

BONNWIT KABRIT UNDER THE STARRY SKY.

BONNWiT hoNeyBee

WiTh youR LULLaBy.

BONNWIT BOURIK AT THE CREEK.

BONNWIT MY CHILD. IT'S TIME TO SLEEP.
NOW CLOSE YOUR EYES WITHOUT A PEEP.

GLOSSARY

Creole Word	Definition	Creole Pronunciation
Bonnwit	Goodnight	*boh•nweet*
Kabrit	Goat	*'kah•breet*
Lakou	Yard	*'la•koo*
Granmoun	Elderly Person	*'gruh•moon*
Chat	Cat	*shot*
Zandolit	Lizard	*'zuhn•doh•lit*
Bannan	Plantain	*'buh•nahn*
Lanmè	Ocean	*luh•meh*
Bourik	Donkey	*'boo•reek*

About the Author

Elizabeth Turnbull was born and raised in Haiti where she grew up surrounded by the sites and sounds brought to life in *Bonnwit Kabrit*. As a young child she would spend hours snuggled in the laps of her parents and older brothers while they would read a story to her. One of her greatest joys was learning to read and having the power to unleash the stories for herself.

Elizabeth went on to study Spanish and Journalism at Wake Forest University and receive her MA in Latin American and Caribbean Studies from Florida International University. Today, she is the Senior Editor for Light Messages Publishing where she believes she is immensely blessed to immerse herself in new stories every day. Elizabeth lives in Durham, NC, with her husband and step-daughter. Together, they are starting a small farm. Perhaps they'll get a goat, and every night they'll say, *Bonnwit*.

About the Illustrator

Erin Vaganos grew up in an underground house her parents built deep in the woods near the NY Finger Lakes. She watches far too many B sci-fi and horror flicks, is fascinated by carnivorous plants and abyssal fish, and loves a good deli and the occasional fried pickle. Now she lives with her husband Anthony, daughter Iris, and dog Juno just outside NYC in a 118-year-old house.

CPSIA information can be obtained at www.ICGtesting.com
Printed in the USA
LVOW02s1145131013

356696LV00010B/17/P

637T13 CP 7270
11/25/13 161170 SCLE